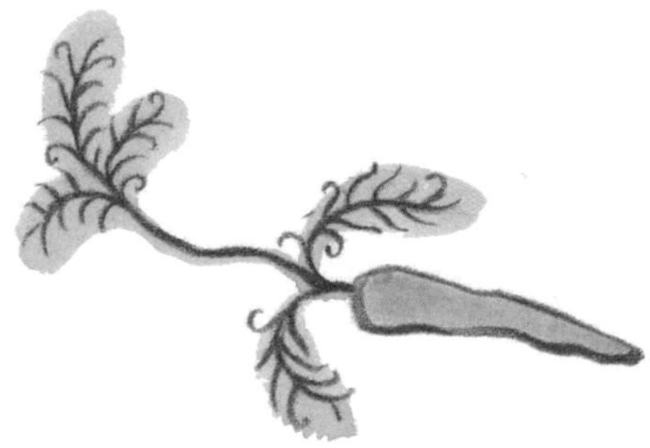

First published in hardback in Great Britain by HarperCollins *Children's Books* in 2018
First published in paperback in 2020

1 3 5 7 9 10 8 6 4 2

ISBN: 978-0-00-818028-7

HarperCollins *Children's Books* is a division of HarperCollins*Publishers* Ltd.

A CIP catalogue record for this book is available from the British Library.

Visit our website at:
www.harpercollins.co.uk

Printed in China

The Rescue of BUNNY WUNNY

Emma Chichester Clark

HarperCollins *Children's Books*

Bunny Wunny
belonged to Imelda.
He was her favourite
fluffy toy.

He was given to Imelda
when she was a tiny baby.

She **never** let him out of her sight.

No matter how many
brave little toys she had...

...Bunny Wunny was the one
she always wanted the **most**.

Imelda's parents **adored** her.

She was the **apple** of their eye…

…the **cherry** on their cherry pie.

They gave her
EVERYTHING
she ever wanted.

And they loved Imelda more than
ANYTHING.

But, sadly, Imelda did not **really** love Bunny Wunny.

She wasn't very kind to him. And there came a day when Bunny Wunny could stand her **no longer.**

He **had** to get **away.**

screamed Imelda.
She nearly yelled
the house down.

Bunny Wunny
shook with fear.

“What’s the matter, Angel Pie?”
asked her father.

screamed Imelda.

So they
searched
high
and
low…

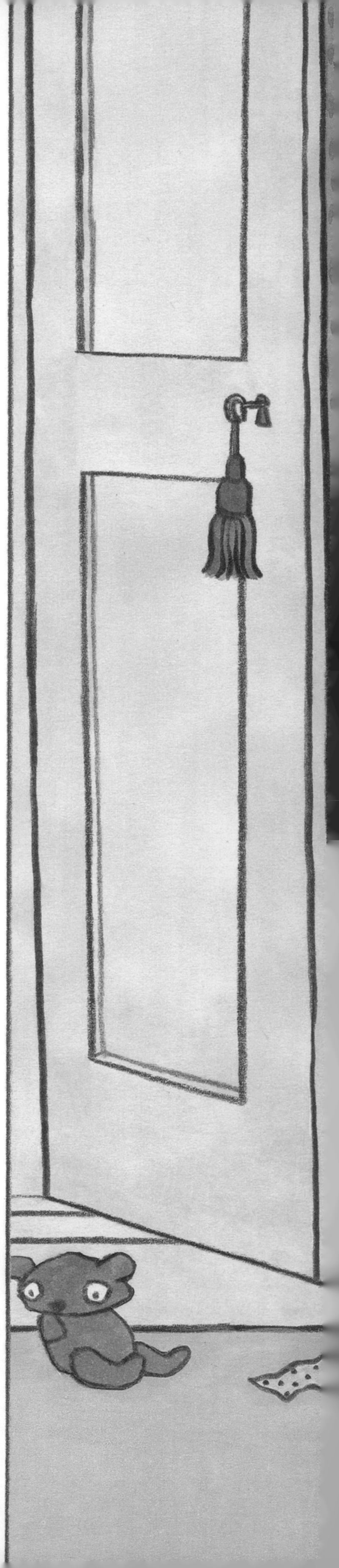

But Bunny Wunny was
not coming out for anyone.

"Let's go to the toy shop
and buy another rabbit!"
said Imelda's mother.

Imelda
yelled.

THE ONLY THING I WANT NOW IS A *REAL* RABBIT!
said Imelda.

So Imelda and her parents went to the pet shop. The nice man smiled at Imelda.

“Can I help you?” he asked.

Imelda bared her teeth.

“I WANT A RABBIT!”

Imelda shouted.

All the rabbits hurried to the back of their pen.

All except one, that is.
It went on quietly eating a carrot…
didn't even look up.

THAT ONE!

cried Imelda.

Back at home, Imelda sat in her room and **stared** at the rabbit.

She **poked** it with her finger but he didn't even turn round.

I DIDN'T KNOW REAL RABBITS WERE SO

BORING!

she said.

You're making
a BIG mistake!

replied the rabbit.

Imelda's eyes opened wide.

The rabbit was suddenly the size of a poodle.

Imelda blinked.

Then the rabbit was suddenly as big as Imelda.

Imelda gasped.

And then the rabbit was
as tall as **her father.**

Imelda screamed.

said the rabbit.

Imelda's parents
popped their heads
round the door.

"Good grief!"
said her father.

said the rabbit.

Imelda snorted
like a warthog.

"That's **our darling!**" said Imelda's mother.

"Our *dearest* darling!" said her father.

asked the rabbit.

"Like her? We *adore* everything about her!" said Imelda's parents.

But she really needs to *change*…
began the rabbit.
"She's perfect!" said Imelda's father.
Wouldn't you like her to be kinder, nicer, gentler?
asked the rabbit.

"We love her just the way she is,"
said Imelda's mother.

The rabbit was quite lost for words.

said the rabbit.

squeaked a little voice. And out hopped Bunny Wunny.

roared Imelda.

Oh no, you don't, Imelda!
Leave Bunny Wunny alone.

said the rabbit.

He grabbed Bunny Wunny and put him safely out of Imelda's reach.

Okay,
said the rabbit,
I'll be going then, if you *really* don't need me?
"Bye, then!"
said Imelda's parents.
GRRRRRRRRRRRRRRRR!
growled Imelda.

called Bunny Wunny.

Are you sure you don't want to be kinder to your toys, Imelda?

asked the rabbit.

But Imelda said nothing.

"Some people will never change,"
said the rabbit.

"No," agreed Bunny Wunny.
"It's a shame it's not a happy ending."

"I'm happy!" said the rabbit.

"Me too," said Bunny Wunny.

said the rabbit.